'To my parents – Yvette & Basil – for a happy childhood.' K.B.

a minedition book

English edition published 2019 by Michael Neugebauer Publishing Ltd. Hong Kong

Text copyright ©2019 by Krystia Basil
Illustrations copyright © 2019 by Laura Borràs
Coproduction with Michael Neugebauer Publishing Ltd., Hong Kong.
Rights arranged with "minedition" Rights and Licensing AG, Zurich, Switzerland.

Michael Neugebauer Publishing Ltd.
Unit 28, 5/F, Metro Centre II, 21 Lam Hing Street, Kowloon Bay, Hong Kong.
Phone +852 2807 1711, e-mail: info@mineditiuon.com
This edition was published simultaneously in Canada.
Printed in July 2019 at L.Rex Printing Co. Ltd.
3/F, Blue Box Factory Building, 25 Hing Wo Street, Tin Wan, Aberdeen, Hong Kong, China.
Typesetting in Skia
Library of Congress Cataloging-in-Publication Data available upon request.

ISBN 978-988-8341-89-4
10 9 8 7 6 5 4 3 2 1
First Impression

For more information please visit our website: www.minedition.com

A Sky Without Lines

Krystia Basil

Laura Borràs

minedition

Arturo loved to look at maps.
He liked seeing all the thick lines that showed where
the different countries met, as if greeting each other in
a tight hug.

But his mother told Arturo the lines on the map were drawn
to stop people from moving freely across the land.

This made Arturo sad.
Because Arturo and his mother were on one side of a line
and his father and Antonio were stuck on the other side.

Antonio was Arturo's brother and his most favorite person in the whole wide world. Antonio had taught Arturo all the important things – how to remove his shoelaces so he didn't have to tie them, how to ride a bike hands-free, how to knee pop a fútbol.

Arturo missed Antonio very much.

Arturo was sure if he looked carefully at the map he would find a gap in the line. He would squeeze through, run fast as his legs could carry him, quickly hug Antonio, and come straight back to his mother.

But the only part without lines was the ocean.
Arturo did not know how to swim.
Antonio had tried to teach him, but instead Arturo had preferred
clambering onto Antonio's back to pretend he was a seahorse.

Arturo dreamed all day and night about meeting Antonio again.
During the day he dreamed with his eyes open.
He dreamed of building a tunnel that went UNDER the lines.

But he worried he might lose his way before he reached the patch of dirt that his mother had swept with a broom, every single day, so he and Antonio could play on it.

Surrounded by frangipani bushes with a small adobe house in the middle, it had been their home.

Sometimes he dreamed of building a bridge OVER the lines.

But at day's end he would stop, tired and sad, wondering why the lines had to be there in the first place.

Sometimes Arturo dreamed when
his eyes closed in sleep.

In these dreams he and Antonio met in the sky.
They flew up, up, up into space and landed on the moon.

There, they played fútbol and picnicked.
Their faces gleamed with smiles, sweat,
and the sticky sweetness of warm churros.

Arturo always awoke from this dream happy, his heart filled with
hope that it would come true. The moon was a long way away,
but he felt sure that when they got there no one would stop him
and Antonio from being together.

Because he had looked hard, and he'd seen no lines in the sky, none at all.

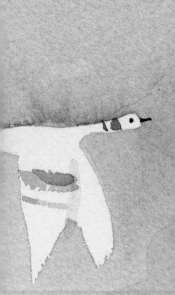